For Qi-meng, my beloved daughter, whose name means enlightenment.
–T.Y.

To my very special aunt who never called me a monk.
–H.C.

Annick Press Ltd.
All rights reserved. No part of this work covered by the
copyrights hereon may be reproduced or used in any form
or by any means – graphic, electronic, or mechanical – without
the prior written permission of the publisher.

Annick Press gratefully acknowledges the support of the
Canada Council and the Ontario Arts Council.

Cataloguing in Publication Data
Ye, Ting-xing, 1952–
Three monks, no water

ISBN 1-55037-443-5 (bound)   ISBN 1-55037-442-7 (pbk.)

I. Chan, Harvey. II. Title.

PS8597.E16T47 1997   jC813'.54   C97-930734-1
PZ7.Y34Th 1997

The art in this book was rendered in acrylic and coloured pencil on gessoed board.
The text was typeset in Tiepolo.

Distributed in Canada by: Published in the U.S.A. by Annick Press (U.S.) Ltd.
Firefly Books Ltd.   Distributed in the U.S.A. by:
3680 Victoria Park Avenue   Firefly Books (U.S.) Inc.
Willowdale, ON   P.O. Box 1338
M2H 3K1   Ellicott Station
                                              Buffalo, NY 14205
Printed and bound in Canada by
Friesens, Altona, Manitoba.

THREE MONKS, NO WATER

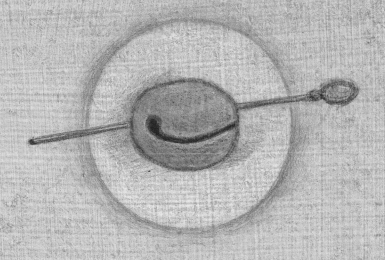

STORY BY
TING-XING YE

ART BY
HARVEY CHAN

ANNICK PRESS • TORONTO • NEW YORK

Once upon a time, there was a mountain; on that mountain, there stood a temple; and in that temple, all alone, lived a young monk.

Besides sweeping the temple, dusting the Buddha statues and replacing the burned incense sticks every day, the young monk would pray, meditate and recite the scripture while beating rhythmically on a wooden block. It was a simple and peaceful life as he followed his vows in the service of Buddhism.

There was no water up in the temple, but there was a clear, cold stream at the foot of the mountain. Each morning, the young monk had to make his way down a narrow, winding trail to fetch water, carrying a shoulder pole with a wooden bucket dangling from each end. On the way down the mountain, the empty buckets danced left and right, right and left, in rhythm with his steps. But on the way back, the pole was bowed by the heavy buckets and it dug painfully into his shoulders.

Rain or shine, hot or cold, dry or damp, the young monk never missed a day lugging his burden up to the temple. With two buckets of water for drinking, cooking and washing, he even had enough left over to start a vegetable garden. But how he wished someone else could help him someday!

One day the temple had a visitor. He was a middle-aged, tall and skinny monk, and his robe was sweaty and dusty from travelling. The young monk offered his tired guest fresh spring water and carefully cooked vegetables from the garden. After the meal, the young monk invited the skinny monk to stay in the temple and be company for him. His new companion accepted gracefully.

The next morning, when it was time to fetch water, they agreed that both of them should go down the mountain together. "That's only fair," they thought to themselves, "since we both will use the water."

But they soon discovered that the carrying-pole was too short to have two buckets placed in the middle while one of them shouldered each end, so they left one bucket behind. Nevertheless, on the way back to the temple they had to stop twice to adjust the bucket. It didn't matter whether the skinny monk was at the front or the back, the bucket would always slide down to the young monk's end and bang painfully against his legs.

"Ow! It hurts!" the young monk whined. "Why are you so cruel to me?"

"I didn't *try* to hurt you," the skinny monk snapped. "Can't you tell the problem is that I'm taller than you are? Don't blame me, blame gravity!"

At the third stop, with almost half of the water having slopped over the rim of the bucket, they marked the centre of the pole and placed the bucket on the line. With the young monk at the back, grabbing the bucket to stop it from sliding towards his companion, they finally struggled into the temple. That day they had barely enough water for drinking and cooking, and none for washing.

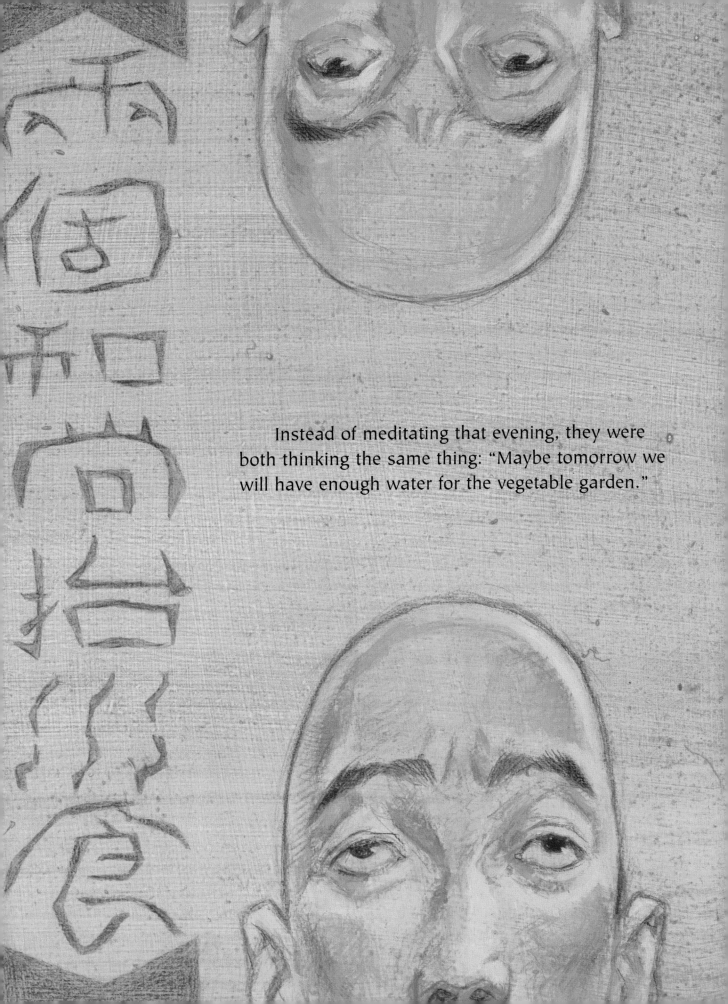

Instead of meditating that evening, they were both thinking the same thing: "Maybe tomorrow we will have enough water for the vegetable garden."

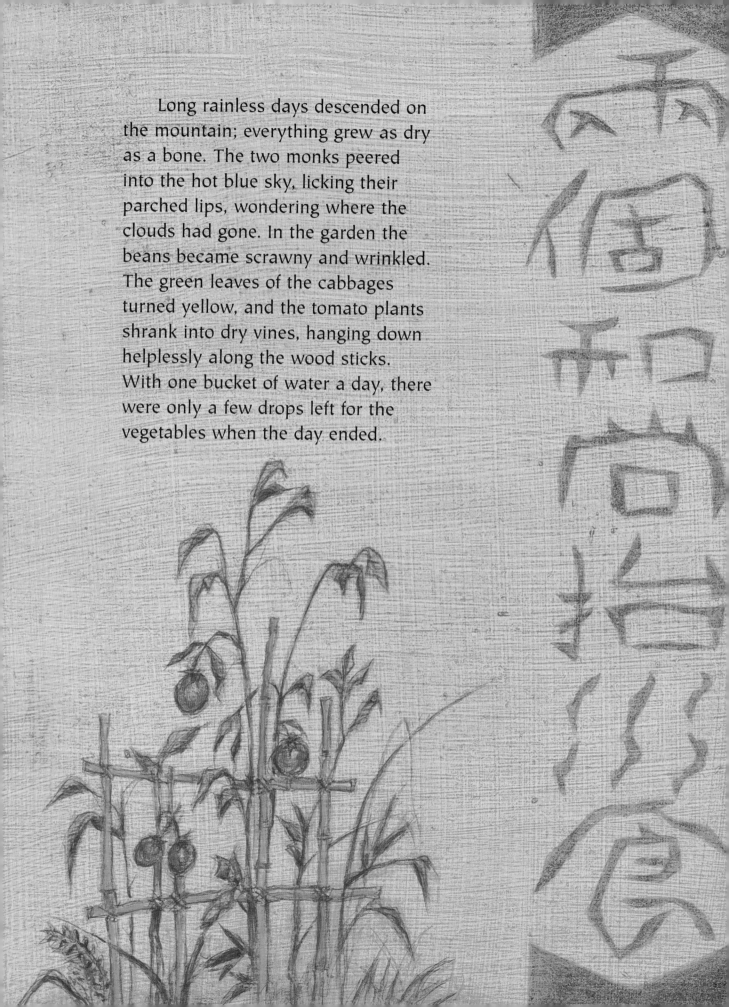

Long rainless days descended on the mountain; everything grew as dry as a bone. The two monks peered into the hot blue sky, licking their parched lips, wondering where the clouds had gone. In the garden the beans became scrawny and wrinkled. The green leaves of the cabbages turned yellow, and the tomato plants shrank into dry vines, hanging down helplessly along the wood sticks. With one bucket of water a day, there were only a few drops left for the vegetables when the day ended.

"How could he be so unreasonable?" The skinny monk peeped at the young one, shaking his head. "He invited me to be his companion and I accepted without hesitation. He doesn't seem to know how to show his gratitude to a person who is willing to sacrifice, especially his senior. He ought to be at the stream now, bringing fresh water up to the temple to show his respect and appreciation."

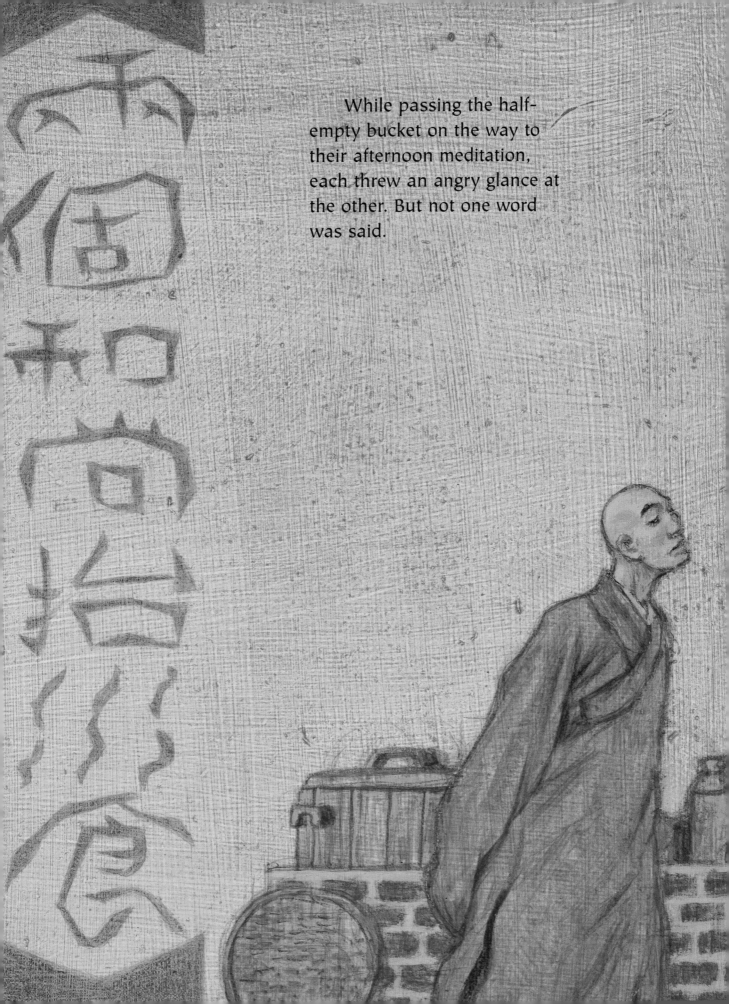

While passing the half-empty bucket on the way to their afternoon meditation, each threw an angry glance at the other. But not one word was said.

One afternoon, the temple had another visitor, a big fat monk, carrying a case full of books. When he was offered a drink, he helped himself to two full bowls. After the meal, he asked his two new friends if he could be of help in the temple and be company for them. The young and the skinny monks stared at each other for a moment, then silently nodded their heads.

While they were beating wooden blocks and chanting scriptures that night, all three of them were thinking to themselves.

"I don't need to carry water any more," the young monk thought with full certainty. "I am younger than both of them, not to mention the fact that they are newcomers. They'd better not forget that taking care of a youngster is one of their commitments. Now, finally, my wish comes true." He almost burst into a smile.

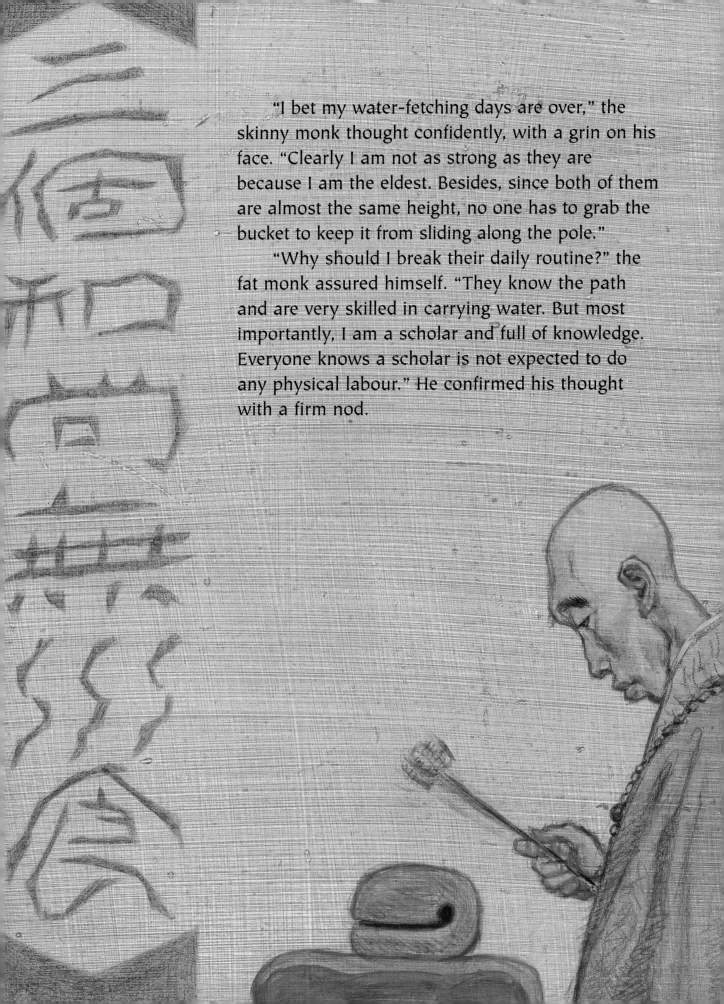

"I bet my water-fetching days are over," the skinny monk thought confidently, with a grin on his face. "Clearly I am not as strong as they are because I am the eldest. Besides, since both of them are almost the same height, no one has to grab the bucket to keep it from sliding along the pole."

"Why should I break their daily routine?" the fat monk assured himself. "They know the path and are very skilled in carrying water. But most importantly, I am a scholar and full of knowledge. Everyone knows a scholar is not expected to do any physical labour." He confirmed his thought with a firm nod.

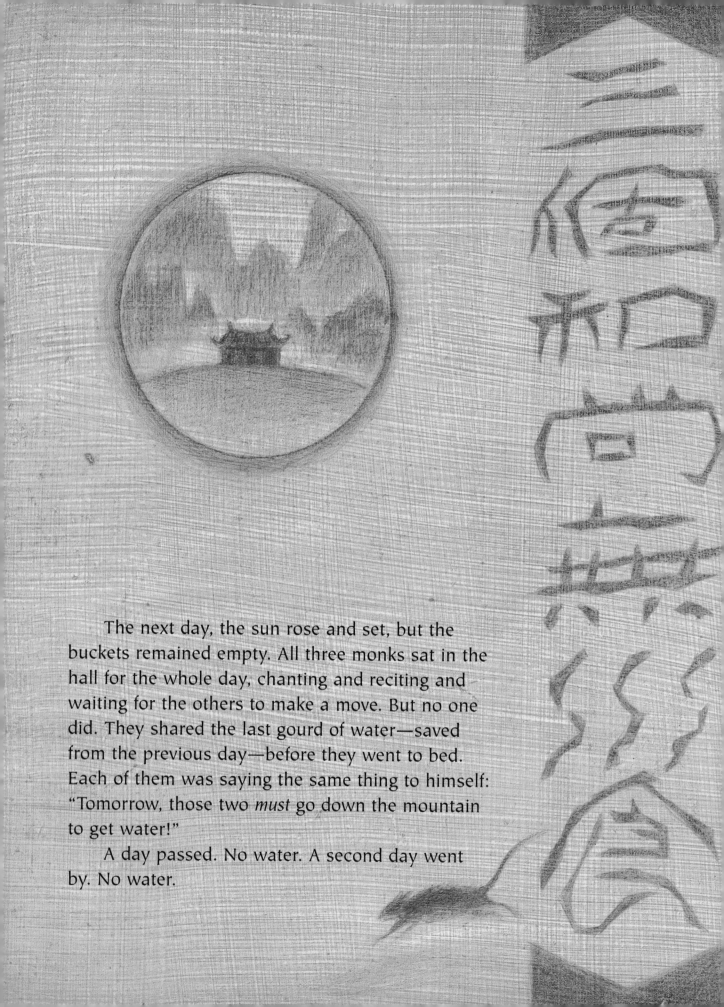

The next day, the sun rose and set, but the buckets remained empty. All three monks sat in the hall for the whole day, chanting and reciting and waiting for the others to make a move. But no one did. They shared the last gourd of water—saved from the previous day—before they went to bed. Each of them was saying the same thing to himself: "Tomorrow, those two *must* go down the mountain to get water!"

A day passed. No water. A second day went by. No water.

Nobody was out of bed when the fourth day arrived. The hall was deadly quiet, and so was the temple. No chanting, no beating rhythms on the wooden blocks.

In the silent temple, a little mouse popped his head from under the drapery that covered the incense table, looking around for food. With his tiny head tilted first to one side and then the other, he listened, and then he crawled up the drapery. As he pulled himself up on to the tabletop, he bumped into a dish holding burning incense sticks, scattering them across the table and on to the floor. As the frightened mouse leapt from the table and scampered away, the draperies burst into flame, and soon the hall was full of smoke.

"Fire! Fire! Fire!" clamoured the young monk, running this way and that in panic.

"Help! Help! Help!" cried the skinny monk at the top of his lungs.

"The buckets! The buckets! Quick!" shouted the fat monk, pointing with both hands.

"Water!" yelled all three of them in unison.

But all the buckets were upside down, empty and dry.

The young monk grabbed the shoulder pole and two buckets and dashed to the mountain path. The skinny and the fat monks rushed into the hall. Choking and coughing, they peered through a sea of black smoke and saw the table blazing. Frantically, they stamped out the fire and dragged the smoking draperies out of the temple. As they hauled out the last one, a stubborn flame came to life again under the table.

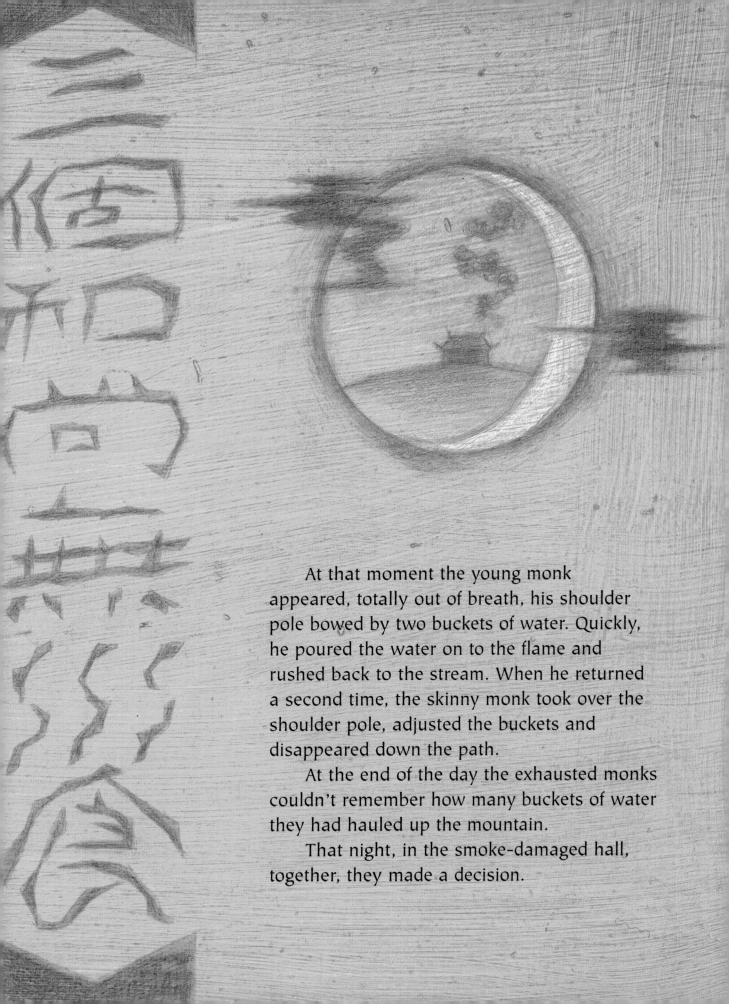

At that moment the young monk appeared, totally out of breath, his shoulder pole bowed by two buckets of water. Quickly, he poured the water on to the flame and rushed back to the stream. When he returned a second time, the skinny monk took over the shoulder pole, adjusted the buckets and disappeared down the path.

At the end of the day the exhausted monks couldn't remember how many buckets of water they had hauled up the mountain.

That night, in the smoke-damaged hall, together, they made a decision.

Early next morning, the three monks went down the mountain-side and brought back a water vat. They installed it outside the temple. Carrying two buckets on his shoulder pole, the skinny monk scooted down and up the mountain to fill the vat with fresh water. The fat monk worked in the hall, moving out the smoke-damaged furniture, cleaning and fixing it.

And the young monk was totally absorbed in attending to the garden, straightening up the vegetables that had survived his neglect and planting some new ones. He made sure that each of them had more than enough to drink. "It's a treat from us," he said loudly to the vegetables, "not just for today, but every day from now on."

A week later, when the three monks gathered at the brimming vat and drank fresh water, they looked at the garden, where the weeds had poked their green leaves out between the rows of vegetables.

The young monk slowly stood up and headed towards the garden. His two friends were close behind.

AFTERWORD

When I was a kid, every time my brothers and sisters and I tried to find excuses for not doing household chores, or passed a work assignment to one another like a relay baton, my mother would always say, "It's typical. Three monks, no water." Years later, I learned that it was an old, widely used expression, with an unknown origin.

—Ting-xing Ye

Illustrator Harvey Chan has rendered the saying in Chinese calligraphy throughout the book. It literally translates to read, "One monk has two buckets of water; two monks have one bucket of water; three monks have no water."

The seal that appears on the inside front and back cover was specially designed to depict the expression *"three monks, no water."* The right panel of the seal depicts "three," the top of the centre panel "monks," the bottom centre "no," and the left panel "water."

Seals are a traditional way to express poetic thoughts or statements. They serve as an artistic signature and supply information about a piece of art or a document. They are used to tell us who the painter or author of a work is, what its title is and even who owned the piece. They are carved in wood or stone and reflect the unique methods and tools of the carver.